A NOTE TO PARENTS

When your children are ready to "step into reading," giving them the right books—and lots of them—is as crucial as giving them the right food to eat. **Step into Reading Books** present exciting stories and information reinforced with lively, colorful illustrations that make learning to read fun, satisfying, and worthwhile. They are priced so that acquiring an entire library of them is affordable. And they are beginning readers with an important difference—they're written on four levels.

Step 1 Books, with their very large type and extremely simple vocabulary, have been created for the very youngest readers. **Step 2 Books** are both longer and slightly more difficult. **Step 3 Books,** written to mid-second-grade reading levels, are for the child who has acquired even greater reading skills. **Step 4 Books** offer exciting nonfiction for the increasingly proficient reader.

Library of Congress Cataloging-in-Publication Data
Hudson, Eleanor. Teenage Mutant Ninja Turtles pizza party / Eleanor Hudson ; illustrated by S. I. Herbert. p. cm.–(Step into reading. A Step 1 book) Based on the Teenage Mutant Ninja Turtles characters and comic books created by Kevin Eastman and Peter Laird. SUMMARY: On their way to get a pizza, the crime-fighting turtles foil a robbery attempt. Includes a pizza recipe.
ISBN 0-679-81452-3 (pbk.)–ISBN 0-679-91452-8 (lib. bdg.)
[1. Heroes–Fiction. 2. Pizza–Fiction.] I. Herbert, S. I., 1935–   ill. II. Eastman, Kevin B. III. Title. IV. Series: Step into reading. Step 1 book. PZ7.H866Te   1991   [E]–dc20
90-53243   CIP   AC

Manufactured in the United States of America   10 9 8 7 6 5 4 3 2

STEP INTO READING is a trademark of Random House, Inc.

Step into Reading

TEENAGE MUTANT NINJA TURTLES®

PIZZA PARTY

By Eleanor Hudson
Illustrated by S. I. Herbert

Based on the Teenage Mutant Ninja Turtles
characters and comic books created by
Kevin Eastman and Peter Laird

A Step 1 Book

Random House 🏠 New York

No sun.

No blue sky.

What a drag.

What should we do?

How about a pizza party?
We all love pizza!

That is a good idea,
my sons.

Mike, you call the pizza store.

Leo, you set the table.

What kind of toppings
do you want?
I want ham.

I want jam.   I want cheese.

I want peas.

And NO anchovies!

The line is busy.

What a drag.

What will we do now?

Do not worry, my sons.
Go to the pizza store.
Bring some pizzas home.
Then we can have
our pizza party.

Put on your coats.

Put on your hats.

No one must know

we are turtles.

So long, sewer!

Hello, street!

Boy, the store is busy!
What kind of toppings
did we want?
I want ham.
I want jam.

Don't shove!
We have to wait
for our turn.
Here, take a number.

Hey, Don.

See that man?

He did not wait.

He did not take a number.

Oh no!

He took a lot of pizzas!

Stop, thief!

Come on, guys!
We can catch him.
SWOOSH...

PLOP!

THUD!

OOPS!

Here is your thief.
May we order
our pizzas now?

One with ham.

One with jam.

One with cheese.

And one with peas.

Sorry.

We are out of ham.

Out of jam.

Out of cheese.

Out of peas.

How about anchovies?

Well, so much for a party—
a party with pizza.

Hello, my sons.

I just saw the news.

You are heroes!

This calls for a party—
a REAL party!

But we don't have
any pizzas.

Don't worry, my sons.
The pizza store called.
They will get more ham,
more jam,
more cheese,
and more peas—
just for you.

But for now—
try these!

Splinter's Easy Pizzas

Sliced English muffin
Tomato sauce
Mozzarella cheese

Toast the English muffin.

Spread each half with sauce.

Top with cheese.

(And ham, or jam, or peas—

or whatever you like!)

Bake in the oven at 400°

until the cheese melts.

HAVE A GROWNUP HELP
YOU WITH THE SLICING
AND THE OVEN.